Care Bear

Busy, Busy, Sunny Day

by Sonia Sander
Illustrated by David Stein

SCHOLASTIC INC.
New York   Toronto   London
Auckland   Sydney   Mexico City
New Delhi   Hong Kong   Buenos Aires

ISBN 0-439-53196-9
CARE BEARS™ © 2003 Those Characters From Cleveland, Inc.
Used under license by Scholastic Inc. All rights reserved. Published by Scholastic Inc. SCHOLASTIC and associated logos are trademarks and/or registered trademarks of Scholastic Inc.

12 11 10 9   4 5 6 7 8/0

Printed in the U.S.A.
First printing, March 2003

It's the start of a busy, busy,
sunny day in Care-a-lot.
"Rise and shine!" calls out
Love-a-lot Bear.

Cheer Bear can't wait to say
good morning to all of her friends.
"Hip, hip, hooray! It's a beautiful day!"

The sun smiles down on the Care Bears,
showering them with sunlit kisses.
Cheer Bear hurries to collect hearts.
"Catch them all!" roots Good Luck Bear.

Tenderheart Bear invites everyone
to join his roller-skating train.
"I hope Tenderheart Bear is watching
where he's going," worries Grumpy Bear.
"Just remember to hold on tight with all
your might!" Share Bear tells him.

Zipping, zooming, round and round they go.

"Special delivery!" says Share Bear. "Yum!" shouts Tenderheart Bear. "Snack time is my favorite!"

All is quiet in Care-a-lot while the Care Bears happily eat their cupcakes.

"Hop on, Wish Bear," says Good Luck Bear. "I'll swing you through the twinkling stars." "Whee!" Wish Bear laughs.

"Do you want to go next, Love-a-lot Bear?"
asks Wish Bear.
"Everyone can have a turn reaching for
the stars," says Funshine Bear.

Soon the sun goes
down.
It's time for best
friends to say good
night.
"I can't wait until
tomorrow," says
Friend Bear.
"Then we can play all
day all over again."

As Wish Bear sends
the first shooting
stars across the sky
she makes a wish,
for another bright
and sunny day.

Bedtime Bear dusts the sky with sweet dreams
for all the Care Bears in Care-a-lot.
"Good night. Sleep tight," says Bedtime Bear.
"The sun will be up and shining again before
we know it."